THE WICKIT

Chronicles
BOOK 4

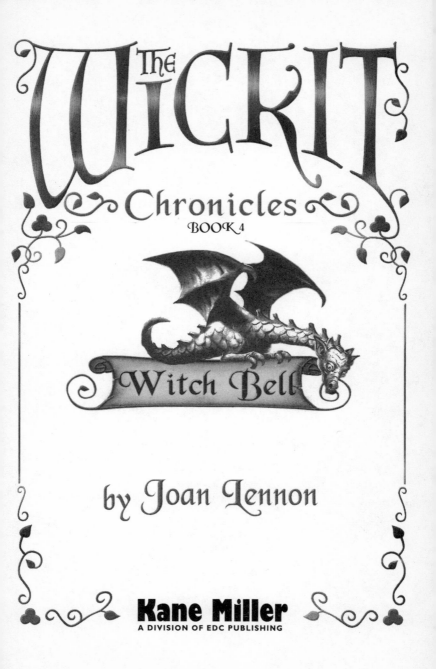

Witch Bell

by Joan Lennon

Kane Miller
A DIVISION OF EDC PUBLISHING

First American Edition 2009
by Kane Miller, A Division of EDC Publishing
Tulsa, Oklahoma

Text copyright © Joan Lennon, 2008
Illustration copyright © David Wyatt, 2008
Illustration copyright © Rowan Clifford, 2008
Design by Ken de Silva
First published in Great Britain in 2008 by Andersen Press Limited

Library of Congress Control Number: 2009922720
Printed and bound in the United States of America
1 2 3 4 5 6 7 8 9 10
ISBN: 978-1-935279-12-9

To my sister Maureen Lennon, in spite of her fears that I won't be able to resist making *"Which Belle?"* jokes in her general direction.

Acknowledgements

I'd like to thank the SAS (Scattered Authors Society) for their help with the Italian song. I'd also like to thank Liz Maude, Anna Bowen and Penny Webber and, as always, my agent, Lindsey Fraser. If there is ever an Olympic event for patience, she's in with a chance at the Gold.

Contents

Brother Gilbert

Prior Benet

Brother Barnard

Abbot Michael

Brother John

Brother Paul

Wickit Monastery

Abbot Michael – The monk in charge of the monastery.

Prior Benet – Abbot Michael's second-in-command.

Brother Gilbert – The Infirmarer, the monk in charge of medical care, including the making of medicines.

Brother Barnard – The Cellarer, the monk in charge of food and provisions for the monastery.

Brother Paul – Wickit's handyman.

Brother John

Pip

Perfect

Perfect

Pip

Walter

Radulfus of Farrow

Blossom

Granny Groan

Walter – the Peddler
The Traveler
Radulfus of Farrow – Special Envoy
of the Church, also known as the
Holy Hunter
The Envoy's serving man
Granny Groan
Blossom

The Traveler

Sometimes it seems as if water wants to take over the world. No more Mr. Nice Guy, no more share and share alike with the land. Sometimes water seems to want it all.

Of course, the medieval Fens were pretty thoroughly damp to begin with – thousands of square kilometers of muddy, marshy bog. The Fen folk lived on islands that were so low lying, some of them were just barely in the air at the driest of times. And spring is never the driest of times. To make things worse, this year there was all the extra snow from the long, hard winter. It had to melt, and it had to go somewhere. Then, there was the rain. Day after day it fell, and the level of the marsh rose. Everybody expects rain in spring, but this was ridiculous! People started to forget what being dry felt like.

Melted snow plus falling rain – there was only one thing that they could add up to in a place like the Fens ...

Flood.

Miracle Under the Moon

The rain had been falling steadily for days, but tonight the clouds cleared away for a while, and a fine, full moon lit the Fens. The Traveler punted along, contentedly humming his favorite song. He was on his way to Ely. He'd heard it was a place where a man who lives by his wits could do well. But he was in no hurry. He would get there when he got there – the stars would show him the way – and in the meantime he was happy just to be a little less drenched.

What was that? The song died away in his mouth, and he let the punt drift to a halt. There it was again!

"A bell?" he wondered to himself.

13

That was what it sounded like, a church bell, the kind that was rung to call the faithful to prayer. The Traveler had thought he was nowhere near any house or hovel or nunnery or abbey – nowhere near any humans at all! – and yet now he was definitely hearing the sound of a bell …

He looked behind him for a moment, trying to judge where the sound was coming from, then turned back – and almost fell out of the boat.

There, clearly visible in the moonlight, something impossible was happening. Something was rising up, out of the middle of the swamp, and it was *enormous*. The punt bucked and threatened to capsize as a wave of black, displaced water swept it sideways into the reeds. The Traveler rammed his pole into the mud and clung to it, staring.

Draped with sedge and dripping with marsh mud, a ruined building was rising up in front of his eyes, taller and taller until it threatened to block out the moon. Once it must have been a church, but now its walls had crumbled, and its spire was a ragged wreck, pointing lopsidedly to heaven. Its roof was gone, its windows were without glass and in its doorway, no door hung. And yet, louder even than the pounding of his heart, its bell was ringing.

"A miracle!" the Traveler murmured in awe.

And then, as the water calmed and the moonlight pierced the ruined walls, the bell ringer stepped out from the shadows and the Traveler screamed …

*W*et Wickit

Pip stood in the pouring rain and walloped the wooden bucket with a stick. It made a horrible, dull, thunking sound. Perfect, the little stone gargoyle hidden in his hood, squirmed restlessly.

"At least you get to cover your ears," Pip muttered. "My hands are too busy *making* this racket!"

"Stop gibbering to yourself, boy!" snapped Prior Benet crossly. He was right behind them, but, what with the rain and the bucket-banging, they hadn't heard him coming.

Fortunately, there wasn't enough time before the service to lecture Pip properly on his many faults (and it really was *very* wet) so Prior Benet left it at that, and swept on into the church.

"Phew," whispered Perfect into Pip's ear, "that was close!"

Pip gave a tiny nod of agreement and, a little shakily, put the bucket away. Then he followed the Prior in to prayers.

It would not be stretching the truth to say that Prior Benet did not like Pip. On the other hand, of course, Prior Benet didn't much like *any*body. He wasn't fond of Brother Gilbert the Infirmarer, for example, even though he was an enormously gifted doctor and knew more about the diseases and cures of the Fenland than anyone else alive. He definitely didn't like Brother Barnard the Cellarer, with his red hair and red face, loud voice and supreme inability to carry a tune. He wasn't any too impressed with Brother Paul, who mended and maintained Wickit's buildings and church and so was beneath the notice of a Prior. And he loathed Brother John, even though Brother John was so incredibly nice he had no clue that he and his dear "brother" Benet weren't the best of friends.

He *respected* Abbot Michael because he was his superior, but he couldn't help thinking he,

Prior Benet, would have been a better choice as head of the abbey than the soft-spoken Welshman. With Abbot *Benet* in charge, Wickit Abbey would be a very different place indeed …

For one thing, it would not include orphan boys called Pip who apparently served no earthly purpose other than to attract trouble. There'd been that embarrassing fuss at Ely a few Easters ago with the young King Arnald. And then that disruptive Norse girl had arrived – and the way the boy disappeared, with no explanation, for all that time – completely unacceptable! And as to what may or may not have happened only this last winter when the Prior had been too ill to keep an eye on events – *that* just didn't bear thinking about!

Well, there was only one thing to be done if Abbot Michael continued to insist on keeping the brat around – and that was to keep him so busy, morning, night and noon, that he wouldn't have *time* to get into any more trouble.

The Devil may find work for idle hands, but so could Prior Benet!

As everyone came out of Prime that morning, it seemed as if all the other Brothers had a similar plan for Pip, though not for the same reason. Brother Barnard, for example, wanted him to gut eels; Brother Gilbert needed medicines made and herbs ground; Brother Paul was going demented trying to fix the leaking roofs on every building in Wickit. Not being a man comfortable with heights, he needed Pip for the climbing and scrambling parts. Knowing this, the others had to admit that perhaps his need was greatest. (The kitchen and the Infirmary were both littered with buckets to catch the drips.)

"It's getting so wet in my Infirmary that I can hardly tell the difference between indoors and out," grumbled Brother Gilbert. "But I want the boy when you're finished with him."

"What about my eels?!" exclaimed Brother Barnard. "Who's going to help me with that gutting?"

But, strange to say, Brother Barnard's loving colleagues, one and all, had disappeared.

"Thanks!" Pip whispered to Brother Paul as they scurried away, and the wiry little monk gave him a conspiratorial wink.

"What's first, then?"

Brother Paul squinted up at the sky. It had stopped raining, for a wonder, but there were more dark clouds low down to the east.

"Best start with the highest and hardest while we've got the weather," he said.

"The church tower?"

Brother Paul couldn't help a shudder, even when he knew he wasn't making the climb.

Pip patted his friend's arm. "Don't worry," he said. "It'll be fine."

Inside his hood, Perfect stirred happily. She loved the church tower. In a way, she'd been born there. She'd been carved out of the stone of the tower for no other reason than the stone carver's joy in his craft. And then no one had seen her until Pip arrived to check the roof all that time ago and heard her sneeze …

As soon as Pip had climbed safely over the low parapet of the tower, Perfect slithered eagerly down his sleeve and hopped out onto the lead flooring.

"I haven't been up here since last autumn,"

she chirped, looking around at her old home all bright-eyed. "Oh, the view!"

"Well, enjoy it," said Pip fondly. "And I'll make sure the lead covering is all right."

It looked to be still in excellent condition. The drainage runnels were clear, and there were no suspicious cracks in the lead. Pip had almost finished his inspection when he heard a small sneeze behind him. He turned to look. There was the "V" that stood for Vincenzi, the stone carver who'd made Perfect and then made his mark to prove it, before going away forever. And there was Perfect, curled into her old place amongst the carved stone flowers and fruit, just as she'd been when Pip saw her for the very first time.

The two grinned at each other.

"How does it look?" Brother Paul's voice drifted up anxiously.

"Don't worry, Brother," Pip called back. "It looks … Perfect!"

"Ooo, very witty!" said the little gargoyle tartly, but he could tell she was pleased.

With Perfect back in his tunic and his feet back on solid ground, Pip was ready to start mending the reed thatch on the other buildings – until Brother Paul discovered, to his disgust, that

Eloise, the Abbey goat, had gotten into his reed store and was enthusiastically eating some while trampling on the rest. They dragged her out (protesting loudly) and returned her to her own shed, where she promptly began to eat the food there too.

"You can see why goats are the Devil's favorite," grunted Brother Paul. "Well, there's nothing for it, Pip. We can't do any more until you take the punt and go and cut me some more reeds."

He explained exactly which reed bed he wanted Pip to cut from, what lengths he needed, and how many armfuls.

"What will you do while I'm gone?" Pip asked.

Brother Paul pulled a sad face. "What choice do I have? I will go and help Brother Barnard … gutting eels!"

Song in the Mist

Pip had cut only part of a boatload of reeds when the wind dropped, the fog came down, and the mist came up. It was at least as wetting as rain, and soon Perfect had droplets clinging to her nose and her wings and the tip of her tail. Pip had started out still damp around the edges and was quickly soaked again, but he had his work to keep him warm. He carried on as fast as he could.

He'd jammed the punt pole into the mud to hold the boat so he could work without scooting himself sideways all the time. But there was still a fair amount of wobbling. Bend, wobble, cut and gather, bend, wobble, cut …

Perfect loved it! First she hung onto the prow,

spreading her wings for balance. Then she got a bit bolder and only held on with three feet, and then only two, and finally she was teetering on one foot with her wings folded along her back.

"Look at me! Look at me!" she kept shrilling.

It was a good game, but after a while outsmarting wobbles stopped being so much fun. The pile of reeds was growing steadily, and when Pip paused to straighten his back and stretched, Perfect hopped up onto his shoulder. She licked a raindrop off his ear.

"This is getting boring," she announced. "Haven't you gotten enough yet?"

Pip smiled. "Almost enough … " but then he realized she wasn't paying attention to him anymore.

Odd as it might seem, gargoyles tend to have really excellent hearing, so it wasn't unusual for Perfect to notice if someone were coming towards them through the reed beds before Pip did. What was unusual *this* time, though, was the way she reacted to what she heard.

From the beginning it had been essential to keep Perfect carefully hidden. The penalties for anything to do with demons or witchcraft were severe, and usually included death. As part of a church building, the little gargoyle shouldn't really be considered demonic, but there was no guarantee the authorities would see it like that. The fact that Perfect was made of stone and could also breathe, talk, fly, swim and be alive – well, even Pip had to admit she wasn't *usual*.

Now, with someone apparently approaching, he expected her to immediately scoot out of sight.

But she didn't. Instead of slipping neatly into Pip's hood or up his sleeve, she *froze*, right there, in full sight, on his shoulder. Pip could feel every one of her sharp little claws digging in.

"Perfect?" he whispered. "What … ?"

And then he heard it too.

Somebody was singing. Out there in the mist, somebody with a fine tenor voice was singing a mournful-sounding song, in a language Pip didn't recognize.

"Hide, Perfect! What are you waiting for?" he urged. "Somebody's *coming*!" He tried to shove his friend backwards into his hood and out of sight – instead, Perfect suddenly tensed all her muscles and did the exact opposite! She launched herself into the air, shrieking at the top of her voice, "My Maker! It's my Maker! *He's come back!*"

and disappeared into the wall of mist.

"What? Who? Where?" spluttered Pip, almost dropping the pole in his hurry to go after her. What was she talking about? Vincenzi, her Maker, was dead, or so Brother Paul thought, and they'd believed him, hadn't they?

He was making so much noise frantically flailing and splashing his way through the reeds that he didn't hear the song break off abruptly in mid-note. He didn't hear the soft whistle of amazement, or the squawk of surprise from Perfect. But then he shoved the punt through one last barrier of rushes and there they were …

… the little gargoyle, looking devastated, as she stared up into the face of a complete stranger.

"Another miracle!" the man said, and sat down with a thud.

He was a young man, handsome, with unruly black hair, wide-open brown eyes and a "you-can-trust-me" kind of face. He was tall and seemed to be full of energy, and every move he made was larger than life and dramatic. Pip could easily imagine him on a stage in front of an audience of kings, instead of sitting in a damp punt talking to a scruffy boy and a sad-hearted dragon.

"You're not Vincenzi, are you? You're not really Perfect's Maker?" asked Pip, though he already knew the answer from the sorrow on the little gargoyle's face. It was a few moments later and he had brought his punt alongside the stranger's so that they could sit facing each other to talk.

"Perfect? Is that your name, little miracle?" asked the man, reaching out a finger to stroke her on the head. Since it was far too late to hide now, the gargoyle was perched on the gunwale of Pip's boat, midway between the two humans. The stranger could hardly take his eyes off her as he answered Pip's question.

"I wish I could say I was the Maker of such a well-named wonder," he said, with regret in his voice. "But, alas, I'm not." And he spread his hands in a wide, dramatic gesture of apology.

Everything the man did was *big*, Pip noticed, as if he had more life inside him than he knew what to do with. But Pip was more concerned about Perfect just then. She, on the other hand, seemed smaller than usual, and all tensed in on herself.

"What made you think Vincenzi had come back?" he asked her carefully.

"It was the song," said Perfect. She sounded so sad.

"The song?"

"Yes, my Maker used to hum that song. It's the first thing I ever remember hearing. It's stupid, but I guess it never occurred to me that anybody else might know it too," she said, and her wings drooped.

"Oh, small Perfect, I am so sorry!" said the stranger. "If I had known it would make you sad, I never would have sung that wicked song. But then *I* would have been sad, because then I might never have met *you*!"

Pip frowned a little, thinking to himself, *You didn't even know she existed, so how could you be sad at not meeting her?* But Perfect had no difficulty accepting the man's words at face value.

"No, I ... I like to hear it. Would you sing it again? For me?" she asked. "I never knew it had words. My Maker always just hummed."

"Of course – I'd be glad to! But won't your family be worrying about you both, out in this bewildering fog? If I'm not mistaken, it's starting to get late ... "

"God's Eyebrows!" said Pip, looking around in alarm at the fading light. "You're right! We'd

28

better be getting these reeds back to Brother Paul – "

"Brother Paul?" asked the stranger quickly. "It's a monastery you come from? Though I should have guessed – something as superbly made as a Perfect could only be part of a great, grand cathedral, am I right?"

Pip and Perfect snorted in unison. No one had ever described Wickit's homely little church, with its stumpy tower and old doors that stuck in damp weather (in other words, that *always* stuck), as "great" or "grand" or anything remotely like "a cathedral!"

"I have made a joke?" the man asked with a smile. "Never mind. Still, they will be worried and wanting to know you are both safe and well. I know *I* would want to know the whereabouts of a boy and a wonder like you – "

"Oh, but they don't know about her – *nobody* knows – you must promise you'll never tell!" cried Pip, and Perfect flapped her wings in agitation.

The man just stared.

"Don't you see?" shrilled

Pip. "There are plenty of people who would think she was from the Devil – who'd want to destroy her! And anyone who'd been in contact with her – even you! – they'd think was likely bewitched. And even though nobody at Wickit knows about her, if the church authorities found out they might not *believe* they didn't know. They might think the brothers were bewitched too, and that Wickit should be closed down forever … You have to swear to us you won't tell."

The man nodded slowly. "Of course," he said solemnly. "You're right, of course. It is astonishing you are able to keep your friend a secret, but it is clearly a serious matter that you continue to do so. I will say nothing. Not a word to a soul. Trust me." And he put a finger to his lips and nodded again with a show of great earnestness. "Let us go now to your monastery where I will admit to the Brothers that I have become totally lost, and beg a night's lodging, eh?" And he stood up and reached for the punt's pole.

"But wait," said Pip. "We don't even know your name!"

"Mostly I try to get by without one!" the man replied cheerfully. "But *you* can call me the Traveler."

Doubts

As Pip led the stranger home, his mind was buzzing. *Can we trust him?* he wondered anxiously. *Why won't he tell us his name? What was he doing out there?* And most important, *Will he say anything about Perfect?*

There was one thing, however, that he wouldn't have to worry about with this visitor. The Abbey was too small to have a proper guesthouse, so usually, overnight visitors to Wickit got to share the floor of the kitchen with Pip. Which meant, normally, that he needed to take extra care to keep Perfect out of sight.

"Well, at least we don't have to worry

if I snore tonight!" the little gargoyle chirped cheerfully. Pip was always amazed when she did that – seemed to know just what he was thinking about. When pressed, she insisted she just looked into his ear and *saw* his thoughts – "as well as a clear view out the other side!" – before dissolving into uncontrollable giggling at her own wit.

"Are we almost there?" the Traveler called from the following punt.

"Yes. The channel's wide from here on – you can come up beside me now," Pip called back. And as the stranger pulled level with him, he pointed ahead. "There it is!"

Wickit's island barely rose above the breeze-blurred water, looking like an over-turned boat that might very soon disappear from sight. But there were clearly places worse off than here. What was left of the foreshore was littered with far more punts than the abbey owned.

"I guess I'm not your only company today!" commented the Traveler.

"People are getting flooded out," said Pip, adjusting the route he was taking in order to land beyond the punt-jam.

"And look! The Walter man is here too!" chirped Perfect, before sliding down inside Pip's hood for safety.

Her sharp little eyes had spotted Walter the Peddler. He was a good friend to Pip. Last winter he'd made him a pair of skates that had stood him in good stead in his race across the frozen Fens to warn King Arnald of Lord Randolph's invasion.

Walter's daughter, her husband and their children were also among those flooded out of their homes. No matter how far the Peddler roamed – and sometimes he was gone for several years at a time – he always ended up in the Fens to see them again. At this time of the year, Walter's pack was pretty empty, since he'd spent the winter off the road and away from the towns. Summer was his traveling time, and he would normally have already been off to buy and sell his way up and down the country. But while his daughter and her family were in danger, he was going nowhere. Except to Wickit, of course.

"Pip!" he called out now. "I was wondering where you'd gotten to! And who's your friend?" he added cheerfully, as he helped haul the two punts up through the mud.

"I … he's not … " There was already a little crowd forming, including most of the brothers. Pip didn't know what to say about the stranger, but the Traveler had no difficulty introducing himself. Being the center of attention didn't seem to trouble him at all. He spoke up at once, loud and clear so everyone could hear him.

"I was on my way to Ely when your lad here found me," he said, and he smiled across at Pip as if they were the oldest and best of friends.

"What were you going to Ely for?" asked Prior Benet suspiciously.

The stranger lowered his eyes and looked attractively humble. "I am on pilgrimage," he said.

"In thanks to God for delivering me from a grave illness."

"What illness was that?" asked Brother Gilbert, immediately interested.

In a low voice that nevertheless carried to every ear, the stranger uttered a single word.

"Plague."

As one, most of the listeners took a step back. Brother Gilbert, however, took a step closer.

"Tell me more," he said. "What were your symptoms? What medical advice did you follow?"

"Are you sure you're really cured?" asked someone from the back of the crowd.

The Traveler's smile was dazzling. "God saved me over a year ago. I will show you." And he pulled his tunic over his head for all to see. There were no swellings or blackenings, nothing to suggest that the most-dreaded of all illnesses had ever taken hold of him.

Brother Gilbert confirmed the stranger's good health. There was still some hesitation on the faces in the crowd – the Black Death was well-known for being virulent and mortal, and it was thought to travel faster than a man could walk. To *survive* the illness, and to be as healthy and strong-looking as this stranger, was not far short of miraculous.

"I think God must have plans for you, friend, to give you back your life like that," said Brother John, with a sweet smile. "And you're welcome to stay with us now. Until the flooding eases up, and you can safely go on with your pilgrimage."

"I thought I'd make a bed for him in the kitchen," said Pip, but Brother Gilbert shook his head.

"All full up there, and until I need the Infirmary for patients, we've housed Walter and his family there."

"Don't worry, we'll find your friend a space," said Brother John reassuringly. Which they did. Though Pip was not certain when the Traveler had become his friend …

Over the next few days, the Traveler got everywhere. He helped Brother Barnard in the kitchen, swapping recipes and telling tales of the faraway spice fields he'd seen on his travels. He argued points of medicine with Brother Gilbert. He helped Brother Paul in his continuing fight against leaks – whenever the rain let up enough. He talked with Abbot Michael about Wales, which he had journeyed through a few years back. He talked to Brother John about whatever floated into the fluffy-haired monk's mind. He even tried to charm Prior Benet – though on this front at least, he had to admit defeat. And, as more and more of Wickit's parishioners arrived, driven out of their homes by the rising flood, he got to know them all and was always ready to lend a hand getting them settled.

He seemed to know just what each person needed and just what would interest them, just what would put a bit more bounce in their step and a smile on their face.

In return, everyone (except Prior Benet) liked the Traveler. He was a very likeable person! Under normal circumstances, Pip would have liked him too. But he couldn't help being afraid. He couldn't forget that this stranger knew about Perfect, and all it would take was one careless word …

"He wouldn't tell on us!" Perfect insisted, but Pip still worried. Was the gargoyle basing her trust solely on the fact that the Traveler knew a song

that her Maker had known? Was that enough?

The Traveler must have sensed Pip's anxiety, because he went out of his way to be nice to the boy. He even came and helped with the eel gutting!

The water level had stayed steady for a few days, and Wickit's expanded population had shaken itself down into a reasonably workable way of living together. Brother Paul had all the help he could want with repair work, and Brother Barnard's kitchen was filled with laughter and busy hands. Brother John spent his time happily with the children, and Abbot Michael was greeted with smiles and "Good day to you, Father!" wherever he went. Pip and Perfect had to be extra careful in the crowded conditions not to let anyone suspect her existence. Not anyone *else*, that is.

The Traveler continued to be everyone's friend, but now another of his talents began to emerge. It would appear that he was extraordinarily good at imitating people. With just a bit of cloth for a shawl or a hat pulled down, he could *become* someone else. He could pitch his voice for high or low, and he had an astonishing talent for capturing quirks or ticks or turns-of-phrase, so that his characters were instantly recognizable and greeted with roars of laughter and delight. Even the ones being mimicked laughed, for the Traveler's imitations, though uncannily accurate, were rarely cruel. More of a compliment than a mockery. (Though his version of Prior Benet was a little tart – and didn't occur when the Prior was present!)

As far as sleeping arrangements went, every spare inch was filled to overflowing. Still, Wickit had room for everyone.

And in the evenings, there was a lot of laughter and singing and practical joking.

Walter was in great demand for his storytelling and his gossip from the wide world. Wherever there was a group gathered, chances were Walter was in the center of it, with tales and jokes and news from beyond the Fens – even though his news was not all that new, since he'd not been away from the marshes since the autumn before. The great freeze, and now the great flood, had kept him off the roads and away from the towns and markets.

But a good storyteller can make magic out of the most familiar material, and Walter was an *excellent* storyteller.

Pip and Perfect especially liked the ones that centered around young King Arnald – juicy stories picked up from a serving-man's brother's friend, who shared all the best bits with Walter when he came to London. One of their favorites was the time Arnald had smuggled an entire flock of chickens into the French ambassador's bedroom in the middle of the night. The poor man woke up to freshly laid eggs in his shoes and chicken droppings in his hair!

One evening, however, Walter told a tale that neither Pip nor Perfect had heard before …

The dormitory that evening was filled to overflowing with flood refugees. The smell of damp wool from their clothes competed with the smell of well-wetted-but-far-from-clean humans.

"Remember when we were last this packed?" asked Brother John cheerfully. "Isn't it wonderful no one's sick this time!"

Prior Benet gritted his teeth. He objected to sharing with all these common folk, and he did not like to be reminded of the great sickness that had brought so many of them to Wickit last winter. (He also suspected that, during his *own* illness, he'd shown some embarrassing weakness. It was possible he may even have said "Thank you" to the brat Pip! It was not a comfortable thing to remember, so for the most part, he chose not to. Fools like Brother John just kept bringing it up!) But even the Prior couldn't resist listening when Walter started his tale that evening.

In honor of the setting, it was a story about a monastery …

Chapter 5

Walter's Tale

"It's never been an easy life here in the marshes," he began, "but there have always been Fen folk, scattered thinly, living off their wits and their skills. Holy men too – they've been a fixture for as long as anyone can remember, living in their communities, eating, drinking" – he waved a full mug appreciatively at Brother Barnard – "praying and caring for the lay people. But some of these monasteries were built in the most remote parts of the Fenland. Not even a few peat-cutters or fishermen lived near enough to be regular visitors. The story I'm telling you now is about one such monastery. It was so isolated and hidden away that there was only one old man – an eel man – who could be considered a parishioner."

"You mean, he was the only person they looked after, the way Wickit looks after us?!" a child exclaimed.

Walter nodded.

"No old man, before or since, ever had so much thought and prayer lavished on the state of his soul. He was the brothers' one lamb, grey and grizzled as he was, and they prayed for him with unstinting concentration until … "

"Until what?" someone asked.

"Until he died. Oh, it was his time, and he passed peacefully. It was a good death, for him. But for the brothers, it was a disaster! Suddenly, they had no focus – well, of course they could still pray for all the *other* souls in the world, and in purgatory, and in hell for that matter, but now it all seemed so … impersonal. That old man had put a face on the world, do you see, that they sorely felt the loss of.

"So, almost without realizing what was happening to them, the brothers fell into despair. Given time, and prayer, they would most likely have gotten better, but before time and prayer had their chance to work, something dreadful happened. As bad luck would have it, just when the brothers were feeling their most hopeless, a witch came by."

The audience gasped. They knew nothing good could come of this. Walter nodded. They were right.

"The witch sniffed … and sniffed … and then a terrible, hungry smile spread across her face. She'd sniffed out their despair and weakness, and it was like the most delectable smell of Brother Barnard's best stew to her wicked nose. She rushed across the marshes on the back of an ensorceled fish to put a spell on them. She arrived at the monastery as the brothers were being called to prayer, so they saw her coming. Horrified, they held up their crosses just as the witch cast her spell, causing it to fly wild and wide. The witch was furious. She went on her way, cursing horribly and gnashing her teeth, unaware that she had, in fact, succeeded. Her spell had bounced off a wall and lodged in the abbey bell. The brothers didn't realize this – they thought they'd had a lucky escape! Then the time for the next service arrived, and the monk in charge reached out his hand and rang the bell … "

"What happened?" someone whispered.

"Well, at first, nothing happened. At first, everything just went on as usual. It was only when, in the fullness of time, the brothers began to grow old themselves and die, that the effect of the witch's misplaced spell became clear.

"As each monk died, he could not be kept in the ground. At the sound of the bewitched bell, he rose up out of his grave and – dead, mind you – joined the others in prayer. This was disconcerting, to say the least, and it just kept happening. No matter how many times the dead brothers were put under the earth, the very next ringing of that bell brought them back again. Eventually the brothers were *all* dead, and there was no one left to keep trying to bury them. Service after service, day after day, the bell was rung and the monks went down on their increasingly bony knees to pray … "

Walter let the horror of the picture settle into his listeners' minds, and at that moment, just by chance, Pip noticed the Traveler. He was sitting close by, and he had an odd expression on his face. Then Walter started to speak again, and Pip forgot everything else.

"Nobody came that way for years and years."

The Peddler's voice was lower, deeper. "Nobody looked after the buildings, so they fell into decay. The face of the Fens changed, as it does, and the low island the abbey had been built on oozed back down into the marsh. The waters covered it, and the reed beds grew over it, but even then, the bell didn't stop. The ghost monks didn't stop.

"But God is merciful, as we all know. Once in every while, when the moon and the tides and the winds are right, mortal folk can *hear* that bell, if they're close enough. And if they're brave enough, and draw closer still, mortal folk can *see* the lost abbey, for it rises up out of the mud and the murk."

"It never does!" someone gasped.

The Peddler raised his hand. "I have not seen it happen myself. I would be lying to you if I said I had. But this is what I've heard."

"But ... will they be cursed forever?" asked Pip.

"No," said Walter earnestly. "As I understand it, the spell will be broken when someone is brave enough to take the bell out of the hand of the ghost monk and muffle it, so that the souls of the brothers can get as far as the gates of heaven at last. Then, of course, it would be up to St Peter whether or not he uses his keys and lets them in. But the chances are good – they've each and every one of them done enough penance to save men who'd engaged in every sin the world has to offer, and these monks had only succumbed to the one."

"And will the old man be there, waiting for them?" asked Brother John.

"The old man?"

"The eel man – their parishioner – will he be there?"

Walter smiled. "I've no doubt he will be," he said. "No doubt at all."

There was a collective sigh of satisfaction as the story came to an end. Then people broke up into groups, preparing for bed and discussing the Peddler's tale. As Pip stood up to leave, he heard a sour-faced woman saying, "Those monks – they were obviously evil. They deserved to be cursed!"

"No," said a voice gently. "Not evil. Just sad." It was the Traveler.

The woman sniffed and turned away, clearly unconvinced. The Traveler had spoken with such authority though, that Pip wondered what he knew. And what had that strange look on his face earlier meant?

"Have you heard that story before?" he asked

quietly, as they left the dormitory and stepped out into the night. "Did you know about the Witch Bell and the monks?"

"Maybe," said the Traveler. He sounded very much as if he didn't want to talk about it, but Pip persisted.

"I couldn't help wondering," he said, "because of how you looked when Walter was telling it. And afterwards, when that woman was saying the monks must have been bad and you defended them. It was almost as if you were talking about people you *knew* … "

"Oh well, you know how it is," said the man. "There's always the temptation to argue with people when they're *so* sure of themselves. And she *was* wrong, so I hope you didn't believe her. You don't want to take everything you hear as gospel, you know."

And suddenly, all the distrust Pip had been trying to squash re-emerged at full strength.

"Does that include what I hear from you?" His voice was harsh, and louder than he'd meant.

The Traveler looked at him, an unreadable expression on his face.

"What do you think I've lied about?" he asked. "Anything specific?"

"*Everything* specific!" cried Pip.

The Traveler made a graceful gesture, inviting him to continue.

Pip took a deep breath. "All right," he said. "Is it really true you had the Plague?"

The Traveler shrugged. "I'm not much of a medical man. I certainly felt quite poorly for a while there, and then I got better. I'm happy to give God the credit for it – and how much more credit would there be if it was the Black Death I'd been struck down with?! The more glory I can pass around, the better, don't you think?"

Pip snorted, then asked, "So, are you really on a pilgrimage?"

"Of course I am, and so are you! *Life* is a pilgrimage!" And he gave Pip a friendly shove with his shoulder.

Pip pulled away angrily. "Have you told us the truth about *anything*?!" he snapped.

The Traveler considered the question calmly. "The truth's a tricky thing, but I'll tell you something I'm almost certain *is* true. Two things, in fact. I've discovered that miracles are true. And I'm pretty sure they come in threes." He grinned at the boy. "I'm curious to see if I'm right about that."

Pip frowned. "I know you call Perfect your

49

second miracle," he said, "but what was the first? You've never told me that."

The Traveler looked steadily at him. "I haven't, have I? It's a story I wouldn't trust to just anyone, but then trust isn't a problem between us, now, is it?"

Pip shifted uncomfortably. Trusting the Traveler was a huge problem, as far as he was concerned!

"So I will tell you," the man continued, "but not now. Not here. Wait until there's a safer moment, and then I will tell you how I stumbled across my first miracle!"

Perfect stirred excitedly in Pip's hood, and somehow the Traveler seemed to sense this. He leaned closer and whispered, *"I will tell you both!"*

Then, with a smile and a nod, he wrapped his cloak around him and walked away.

But before Pip and Perfect had the chance to hear what the Traveler had to tell, someone else arrived at Wickit who would change everything …

Chapter 6

New Arrival

The next afternoon, when Pip and the Traveler were just pitching some buckets of fish guts into the marsh, a punt Pip didn't recognize appeared from behind a reed bed and headed for the Abbey. They stayed to see who the new arrivals were. They weren't the only ones who were curious, either. By the time the boat nosed ashore there was quite a crowd gathered.

Many hands helped draw the punt up the foreshore, Brother John's among them, though he mostly got in the way.

"Welcome!" he cried, greeting the two strangers with equal pleasure. But it was not the man with the pole who had everyone else's attention. It was his passenger.

Afterwards, no one could quite remember their first impressions or say for certain if the man was short or tall, or what he was wearing. All anybody had really noticed were his eyes. They were black and terrifyingly blank and he used them like a weapon. As he scanned slowly from one face to the next, he instantly made each person feel as if they were being pinned, ruthlessly dissected and mercilessly judged. Old guilts and long-past mistakes rushed to every mind. No one seemed able to hold that gaze for more than a moment without being overwhelmed by feelings of having sinned. Pip, along with the others, fought hard against an urge to run away, fast, before he could be accused of anything. Perfect picked up on his fright and burrowed deeper into his hood, shivering.

But no accusation followed. The man, apparently satisfied with his effect on the general bystanders, turned to Brother John.

"I will see your Abbot now," he said. His voice was like his eyes – cold, dark.

Of anyone on earth, Brother John was the least likely to have a guilty secret on his conscience, but even his innocent face looked a little troubled as he led the stranger away. The serving man followed with some bags.

"Who *was* that?!" murmured Pip, turning to the Traveler. But the Traveler didn't answer. He was nowhere to be seen.

That evening, in the dormitory, Pip was handing out extra straw for the pallets when Abbot Michael appeared in the doorway, a bundle of blankets under one arm.

"Good evening! It seems I will be sleeping here, with you all."

There was an immediate chorus of "Here, Father!" "Take this bed, Father!" and a general, eager shuffling to make room. Abbot Michael was well-loved by his flock.

Prior Benet bustled over, frowning indignantly. "This hardly seems appropriate, Father! Why aren't you using your own rooms? As the highest ranking among us – "

But the Abbot interrupted him. "A Special Envoy of the Church outranks everyone, my son, and that is what the floods have brought us today!" Everyone clustered around Abbot Michael, looking for explanation and comfort.

"What's a Special Envoy?"

"Are we in trouble, Father?"

"What does he want?"

"What's brought him here?"

It was the Brothers who were asking the questions, but Abbot Michael raised his voice so that everyone could hear the answers.

"The flooding is what's brought him here, like so many others," he said reassuringly. "He was on his way to Ely but decided, sensibly, that with the water still rising and so many of the usual landmarks submerged, he would stop here instead of getting completely lost."

"Who *is* he, Father?" asked Pip.

"He is Radulfus of Farrow, Special Envoy of the Church. That means he has particular duties to perform, given him by his bishop, to whom he reports. What *exactly* those duties are is nobody else's business and best not speculated on. All we need to know is that he was on his way to Ely and he will be staying with us until the flood waters subside and he can continue his journey safely." The Abbot then started to unroll his blankets, as if to suggest that the topic had been covered, and was now closed.

That may have been what the Abbot hoped for, but it wasn't what he got.

There was a restless reshuffle of bodies, and Walter the Peddler came forward. "This Radulfus – I've heard of him, Father," he said. "There are stories about him the length and breadth of the land, terrible, terrifying stories. They say he can read all your sins just by looking at you – and if he decides to bring you to account for them, well, you can run to the ends of the earth but he'll never stop chasing you. Folk call him 'Envoy' to his face right enough, but behind his back they call him the *Holy Hunter.*"

Abbot Michael was a tolerant man, and he had a genuine liking for Walter, but just at that moment he could have done without the Peddler's love of drama and gossip.

"Thank you for that, my son," he said rather dryly, "but since we won't *be* discussing our guest behind his back, it is not information we're going to need. Is it?" He looked sternly around, and of the man he'd been trailing, the man with no name. He'd been so close this time! So close! He'd finally caught up with him at that last town, but somehow, in spite of all the Envoy's care and zeal and righteousness, the wretch had changed his appearance yet again and slipped away. He'd probably reached Ely by now – all the evidence suggested that would be his next destination. And yet here *he* was, Radulfus of Fallow, the one they called the Holy Hunter, stuck in this no place while his quarry was, perhaps at this very moment, thinking of *him* and laughing. Laughing and planning his next fiendish fraud …

The night was filled with the sound of rain as it fell, steady and uncaring, out of a clouded sky. But the Special Envoy of the Church didn't hear it. It was drowned out by the sound of that laughter in his brain.

Chapter 7

The Envoy's Nose

Radulfus of Farrow trusted his nose. It had never misled him. It was as if he'd been born with the ability to sniff out wrongdoing. There was an awful lot of wrongdoing around, of course, but the Special Envoy was just that – *Special* – and he had no interest in little, *ordinary* sins. It was only the really juicy sins, the ones that involved demons or witches or even the Evil One himself, that normally got *his* nose twitching.

So it didn't make any sense at all that his nose should be twitching now! What of any importance could possibly go on in such an insignificant, back-of-beyond sort of place as this? It was so primitive, they didn't even have a bell to call them to their prayers. They had a bucket, for Heaven's sake, and they bashed at it with a stick! His mind told him there could be nothing here worthy of his consideration – but his nose said otherwise.

Something's wrong here, said his nose. *Something is definitely and distinctly not right.*

And when the Envoy's nose spoke, the Envoy listened.

"What's the matter with you?" Pip asked the Traveler the next day. "You're as restless as a flea!"

"What? I'm not restless," the man replied, trying to look relaxed though his eyes kept darting from side to side.

Pip snorted. "Oh no. Of course not. You only disappear into thin air every other second."

The Traveler looked at him and then half-smiled. "All right. I admit, I am a little edgy. It's just that Wickit's new guest … "

"The Holy Hunter?" Pip's eyes went big. "You *know* each other? Why don't you want to meet him, then?"

"Would you believe it's because I'm shy?" the man asked with a smile.

"No!" laughed Pip.

"No, well, fair enough. He and I have some history. Which I have no intention of telling you about just now, so your ears can stop flapping."

"He's after you?" asked Pip, ignoring the crack about his ears. "Everybody's been saying he's trailing somebody and that he never gives up. Are you really enemies?"

The Traveler spread his hands. "*I* hold a grudge against no man," he said. "Sadly, however, the same cannot be said for the Envoy."

"And you prefer not to remind him of anything you've done that he might be cross about?"

"I prefer not to have him know I am here at all!" grimaced the Traveler. "So now you have a secret to keep for me! That makes us equal, wouldn't you say? And perhaps you will feel a little better, now that that is the case?"

He looked at Pip with an expression that was part shrewd, part rueful.

And he was right. Pip did feel better!

Chapter 8

Storm Warning

Another storm was coming – a big one. All morning, as the Brothers and the other residents of Wickit went about their work, they kept glancing up anxiously at the sky. By midday there was a mass of angry-looking clouds beginning to build on the horizon and it looked as if it might be coming their way.

An impromptu committee gathered around the church door at the end of the service to speak to Abbot Michael.

"It's the Potter family over westwards, Father, and some of the others," said a walnut-skinned peat-cutter. "If that storm comes and it's half as bad as it looks to be, I don't think they'll last it. Their land has got more height than most of ours, and that's a fact, but Wickit's higher still and one more big dump of rain – well, saving Your Honor, I don't even know if *you* won't be flooded out!"

Abbot Michael nodded solemnly. "So why haven't they come already, do you think?" he asked. "They can see the sky as well as we can!"

There was a bit of foot shuffling, until somebody plucked up the courage to say, "Don't be cross, Father, but with the Potters it's because of that disagreement last year with Godfrey and his lot over the peat rights. I know you told them to share and share alike, but they haven't quite seen their way to it yet. And since Godfrey's family is already here, the Potters don't want to come ... "

"But it's not just them, Father," one of the women spoke up. "There's that couple from over Blackwater way as well. Young Agnes is due to give birth any day now. It's her first, and she'd be wanting to stay put."

"And John Fowler's got his father with him, and the old man's dead set in his ways. *We never went a-running to the Brothers every drop of rain in my young days, and I'm not starting now!*" Her imitation of a querulous codger was met with rueful appreciation by those who had elderly parents of their own to deal with.

"Well then, is there time left to go and get them – all of them – safely here before it breaks?" asked the Abbot.

There were some mutterings and calculatings and disagreements, but the general opinion was that yes, there should be time. Volunteers came forward to make the various runs.

"And somebody better go for Granny Groan as well … " added Abbot Michael.

"I'll do that," volunteered Walter the Peddler.

" … not forgetting her goat, of course," the Abbot finished, with an unsuccessfully hidden grin. "She's unlikely to want to leave it behind."

"Oh no!" moaned Walter, who had forgotten the goat.

Everyone knew Granny Groan. It was as if she'd always been there, wrinkled and smiling, and as she was so familiar, nobody noticed any more how inappropriate her name was. Because a more cheerful, sprightly, energetic old biddy would be hard to imagine. Even after her eyesight began to go, she remained relentlessly chirpy. And to complete the mismatch, she was utterly devoted to her similarly long-lived nanny goat, Blossom.

And *Blossom* was the foulest, most bad-tempered, unmitigated harpy of a goat to be found from one end of the vast Fens to the other.

"God speed to you all now," said Abbot Michael. "And a special blessing on you, Walter – I expect you'll need it!"

With a sprinkling of laughter, the crowd dispersed. Pip went with the others to see the rescuers off. Baa-ing noises speeded Walter on his way, and the last they saw of him, he was good-naturedly shaking his fist at them all before disappearing into the reed beds.

The business of the abbey carried on throughout the long afternoon, but everyone had half an eye on the sky and half an ear on the rising wind. By None, the first of the rescuers were returning. Looking very tight around the mouth, John Fowler helped his father out of the punt, while the old man complained in a loud, scratchy voice, *"I said we should have come days ago. In my young days we always came to the Brothers before the house was knee-deep in marsh water ... "* Young Agnes was brought in soon after, white-faced and biting her lips. She was immediately surrounded by a crowd of women who whisked her away to Brother Gilbert's Infirmary, from which several families, the good Brother himself and a number of chickens were evicted.

More stragglers arrived on the skirts of the storm – even the feuding Potters – until there was finally no one left unaccounted for … except Walter, Granny Groan, and Blossom.

"They should be here by now," someone worried.

"It'll be that wretched goat," muttered someone else. "She'll be slowing them down with her fussing over it."

"Maybe Granny didn't understand that she needed to hurry. With her eyesight so bad, maybe she didn't realize the danger?" said a third.

"Or else maybe our good friend the Peddler got lost." Everyone turned to see who had spoken. It was the Traveler. "He doesn't know the Fens as well as the rest of you, and you said yourselves that many of the usual landmarks aren't visible anymore. Under water, like so much else."

Anxious looks were exchanged. They wanted to disagree, but it was all too likely. By now, visibility was very poor and the wind kept veering around, blustering first one way and then another. Keeping on course would be hard, even if the punter was clear what that course should be.

"All we can do is pray," said Abbot Michael, with a worried sigh. He turned to lead the way towards the church when the Traveler took his arm.

"By all means, Father, we can pray," he said urgently. "But we can do more. We can try to guide them to us. We can be the landmark they've missed." And he pointed upward, to Wickit's stubby tower. "Light a beacon, up there, and it'll help them home."

"I've climbed it before, Father," began Pip, as the sky opened and the rain struck in angry, deafening sheets. There was a general rush for the church, as the monks and the refugees ran to get under cover.

"There's no hope of lighting anything in this!" Abbot Michael shouted over his shoulder.

And then there was only Pip and the Traveler, facing each other, wiping the rainwater from their eyes.

"She could do it," the man said, and Pip knew exactly what he meant.

Chapter 9

The Teeth of the Storm

There was no time to waste.

"I'll get the ladder," Pip yelled. "You get a brazier and kindling and wood!" The Traveler nodded, and left at a run.

They met in the lee of the church, but even here the storm made it hard to get the ladder up against the wall. Precious time was lost securing the base of it in the slippery mud. Fortunately Pip knew where there were some large stones, and they were able to wedge the feet of the ladder with them. They paused for a moment, squinting upwards into the darkness with the rain slashing down and the ladder shuddering in the wind.

Brother Paul would really hate this! thought

Pip as, one-handed, he started up the rungs. He had the brazier clutched under his other arm. The Traveler had a load of fuel crammed into a bucket to encumber him. The wind was doing everything in its power to make them lose their grip, and the final scramble up the slick slates and over the tower parapet was a frantic act of faith. But, somehow, they made it.

By now, the storm was almost directly overhead. Lightning flashes seared images of the wind-thrashed marsh on their eyes, images that lasted for long seconds after the darkness fell again, and the thunder boomed. The noise made it hard to think except in little, breathless bursts. Pip found he could only focus on one thing at a time, one step at a time.

"And here I thought monastic life was boring!" the Traveler bellowed, as they struggled to set up the brazier, then piled it high with kindling and wood. Pip grinned back wildly. Perfect's small face showed from inside his hood. She wasn't coming out one minute sooner than she needed to, but he could feel a hugely comforting warmth coming through his shirt as she stoked up the fires inside herself, ready to ignite the wood.

"If this works, we'll need more fuel," the man

shouted, reaching for the bucket he'd brought the first load up in, but Pip shook his head.

"Get more wood, but leave the bucket. I can use it to bang on. Maybe I can make them hear me if the wind dies suddenly." It was no more than a forlorn hope, but the words seemed to stop the Traveler short. For a moment he just stood there, staring at Pip. He looked as if he were having an argument with himself, then shrugged.

"I'll be back," he yelled above the storm, and disappeared down the slick slates so fast Pip was afraid he must have fallen. He leaned anxiously over the low parapet, but there was no way to tell for sure in the screaming darkness. Then another flash of lightning lit up the yard far below, and he saw the Traveler in mid-stride. He seemed to be heading for the dormitory, but Pip had no time to wonder why.

"All right, Perfect!" he yelled. "It's your turn now!"

He'd thought he would hold her in his hands to direct her, but she was much too hot now for his bare skin. Instead, she dug her claws into the cloth of his sleeve and leaned as far forward as she could, to get as close to the wood, and as far away from Pip, as possible. Then she let rip. Her stored-up flame hit the wet wood with a roar and an explosion of steam that made both of them leap back in surprise. But almost immediately the rain had battered down the steam, and they were able to see the brazier.

There was a definite glow there, but it was already dying away in front of their eyes. Perfect flamed again, and again, and the glow deepened its color … and finally, against all likelihood, it flowered into undeniable fire. Pip added more fuel; Perfect moved around the brazier adding more encouragement, and at last the beacon was well and truly alight, sending fiery tongues up into the night.

"They must be able to see that!" cried Pip excitedly. "They must!"

Perfect grinned wildly and went on flaming, while Pip picked up the now-empty bucket and began to bang on it, as hard and as loud as he possibly could. He stamped his feet in time to the beat, just to try and warm up a little. Then the stamping turned into hopping and the hopping turned into leaping and all at once Pip was dancing around on the top of the tower, shouting and banging his bucket like a crazy thing. Between flamings, Perfect added her own shrill cries of defiance, while flying choppy little flights around Pip's head.

The two were so engrossed in their wild dance they didn't notice the Traveler come back. But suddenly, there he was, with a basket of more wood tied to his back … and a bundle under one arm.

They stopped, looking questioningly at him, but he was too windblown to speak. Instead he handed the bundle over, gesturing to Pip to open it. Perfect gave an extra strong flame to the wood to keep the beacon going, and came and perched on Pip's shoulder to see what was inside.

Pip unrolled the rain-drenched layers of cloth. At the last minute, the thing inside almost fell out of his hands, making a muffled, clanging sound. The Traveler reached over, dragged some more cloth from inside, and put Pip's hand on the wooden handle.

"Sometimes you really just need a bell!" he panted, before heading back down again for more fuel.

What the Hunter Saw

Radulfus had retired early that night. He had no interest in the rescue attempts – all this fuss about a few peasants seemed quite unnecessary.

When the storm hit, he'd closed the Abbot's rooms up tight and done his best to ignore the hubbub. Then, without warning, the wind grabbed hold of the shutters and slammed them open, snuffing the candles and filling the room with clamor and confusion. Stumbling across the floor in the howling darkness, Radulfus struggled with the heavy wooden shutters, trying to wrestle them shut again. The rain stung his eyes and soaked his clothes, but he had succeeded in re-fastening the first section when a flash of lightning suddenly lit up the church opposite and burned the image of something impossible into his brain. There, for that brief instant, frozen in the metallic glare, he had seen a figure. Two figures. Two figures and some sort of animal. And, unlikely as it might seem, they were up on top of the church, standing on the stubby tower that stuck so inelegantly from its roof.

The shutters were forgotten as he stared and stared into the night, waiting for another lightning flash to show him what devilry was going on. What else could it be, on a night like this, in a place where no sane mortals would be? The Holy Hunter's nose twitched like a wolf's, scenting prey.

And then something even *more* impossible occurred.

Fire leapt up from the stones of the tower. It couldn't be natural fire, for the rain was sheeting down from the sky as if dumped out of a bucket. No flint could raise a spark in such rain; no wood could catch alight in such a deluge.

Hellfire! thought the Envoy.

It could be nothing else.

In the light of that unnatural fire, the Envoy could see that now there was only one figure visible, and it was small, almost like a child. Steam hissed and billowed and was blown away, but what he had taken for an animal or bird was revealed to be an imp – a miniature devil that was breathing out flames and keeping the hellfire burning brightly. The child-sized demon began to dance, leaping and flailing around. It was shocking, horrible – then, when the other devil reappeared, it got worse. Instead of just dancing, the small devil began to ring a bell. The Hunter knew about such bells. They were known as Witch Bells, and the servants of the Devil used them to call up their Master …

Suddenly his attention was distracted. A shout came from somewhere out in the dark marsh. A light – it looked as if it came from a lantern – was wobbling around out there. The shout came again and was joined by some grumpy baa-ing. The demons on the tower must have heard the sounds too, for they paused abruptly and then disappeared.

The Holy Hunter turned away from the window and left the room, heading decisively into the night.

He had seen enough. He knew what to do.

"Is it them?" asked Perfect anxiously. The wind and the rain were dying down now, but it was still hard to see any distance.

"Stay here," Pip said. "I'll go and find out what's happening."

Stuffing the bell into his tunic for safekeeping, he began the slippery descent, just as the Brothers and their flock came hurrying out of the church below. By the time he'd made it to solid ground, the foreshore was covered with torchbearers, lighting the missing boat's arrival. It was them! Granny Groan, looking tinier than ever in her storm-soaked shawls, was lifted out by many gentle hands and hurried off to the kitchen for some warmth and food. Walter was surrounded by Brothers and friends, all eager to hear his story. Even Blossom the goat was getting a royal welcome.

"Was that you, lad, up on the tower?" Walter was swaying on his feet with exhaustion, but he still managed a wide, warm smile for Pip. "I thought we weren't going to make it – if it hadn't been for the beacon and the bell, I tell you the truth, I could no more have found my way here than I could fly. I was blinded by the rain and deaf with the wind and the thunder – and that wretched goat yelling its head off! – and though Granny bailed like a woman half her age, we were filling up fast, and nowhere to land ... well, all I can say is, bless you, boy! God bless you!"

"But He won't," said a voice. "God has no blessing for the minions of the Devil."

The crowd gasped, and turned to see who could have spoken.

It was the Holy Hunter. And he was pointing at Pip.

Chapter 11

Accused

"Search him!" cried the Hunter. When no one moved, he stepped forward himself, and immediately discovered the bell stuffed inside Pip's tunic. He dragged it out and, being careful not to let the clapper sound, he brandished it in the boy's face.

"Where did you get this abomination?"

"W-what?" stuttered Pip.

"This summoner of Satan, this Witch Bell – where did you get it?" the Envoy demanded.

Pip's brain leapt around, desperately looking for an answer. He couldn't tell the truth – that the Traveler had given it to him – he'd be handing the Traveler over to the Hunter! – but what else could he say? *Hurry up! Hurry up!* his mind shouted. *If you don't speak soon he'll know you're lying!*

"I found it!" Pip blurted. "Sticking out of the mud – by the best reed bed!"

As soon as he'd spoken, he knew no one there believed him. His hands were sweating, and he didn't dare look up because he knew what he would see in every face.

Disappointment, anger, glee and pity …

Pip, how could you? After all we did for you?

I knew it – he was a liar all along! And worse!

One of the Devil's own …

Pip felt the tears forming in his eyes. He'd never felt so alone in all his life.

"Don't bother lying to me," the Hunter said. "I know everything already." His voice suddenly dropped to a vicious whisper, and his dark eyes narrowed. "*I saw you.*"

"We saw him too," said Walter, greatly daring. "He was up on the tower, guiding me and old Granny to safety." Abbot Michael came and stood beside him, his kindly face furrowed with concern.

But Radulfus paid no attention to the Abbot. Instead, he fixed his black eyes on the Peddler. "You saw him," he said slowly. "With a fire. In the pouring rain, when no natural fire could possibly stay alight. You heard him, ringing a bell magicked out of thin air – a Witch Bell, rung to call the Devil … "

Walter faltered. "I didn't see any Devil. I couldn't see much. Just the beacon, that showed which way to go. And the bell. I could hear the bell."

"Does Wickit have a bell?"

"No … not that I … someone … Pip says he found it!"

"You think that the boy lit the fire and rang the bell to help you find your way."

"He *did* help us find our way!"

The Envoy waved this aside. "That's unimportant. It wouldn't have been the first time some incidental good comes out of the actions of the evil ones."

"Who're you calling incidental?" muttered Walter, but Radulfus had lost interest in him now. He addressed the entire shocked and uncertain crowd of Brothers and Fen folk in his dark, cold voice.

"Understand this," he said. "The fire was not lit for anyone of this world. The fire was devil-fire, and the bell was something I have heard of but hoped never to see – a Witch Bell. You can thank God, every one of you, that you did not see what I saw. The fire and bell, the unnatural ferocity of the storm, the barbaric dance, the fire-breathing imp – the signs were crystal clear. This boy was summoning his Master."

"His Master?" Abbot Michael asked.

"He was summoning the Devil. You all witnessed how, as soon as the fire and the bell stopped, the storm did too. The Devil had been and gone again. No doubt he sensed my presence and dared not stay."

"But, Envoy," cried the Abbot, "we've known Pip from a baby – he's no more a servant of the Devil than I am!"

There was a murmur of agreement, but Radulfus only shrugged.

"It is enough that I saw him," he stated, unmoved.

"You can't convict him without a trial!"

"Of course not. The trial will be at first light. I will conduct it. Meanwhile, it would be prudent to put the prisoner in chains," said the Envoy. "Have your Prior see to it."

Everyone turned and stared at Prior Benet, who looked embarrassed and mumbled something.

"What was that?" snapped the Envoy.

"We don't have any chains!" Prior Benet repeated, this time much louder than he'd meant to.

The Envoy looked pained. "What *do* you have?" he asked.

There was a pause. Incarcerating people was not something Wickit did much.

"We could put him in the goat shed," offered the Prior tentatively.

"If that is the best you can do. My man will stand guard 'til dawn," said Radulfus, and walked away.

So Pip was shut in with Eloise and Blossom. They were warm, and welcoming, but he longed for Perfect. He was well aware of how much worse things would be if the Hunter had found her on him, but his need for her now was so great it drowned out all the other feelings of fear and shock …

As he slumped in the straw, a warm goat chewing cud on either side of him, he didn't realize that a silent shadow was moving across the Abbey yard towards his prison. So quiet was the shadow that Blossom and Eloise didn't even twitch when it crept through the door and closed it soundlessly.

It was only when the Traveler sat down beside him, and Perfect's sharp little claws dug into his shoulder, that Pip realized he was no longer alone.

Chapter 12

Whispers in the Dark

"How did you get in here?! I thought the Envoy's serving man was standing guard!" Pip exclaimed, as he stroked Perfect's hard little head.

"That's right. He was," said the Traveler, lighting a horn lantern. "He still is! Although, since Brother Gilbert gave Brother Barnard some ground poppy seeds to put in his ale, he's not so much standing guard as *sitting* guard. In a slumped, asleep sort of way. I don't imagine he'll be telling his master about that, though."

"So what are we waiting for?" chirped Perfect impatiently. "Let's get Pip out of here!"

The Traveler said nothing, but Pip shook his head. "We can't," he said. "I'd get Abbot Michael and the Brothers into a lot of trouble if I escaped now."

"You're right," said the Traveler. "The blame would fall on them – the Envoy might even have a case to close the monastery down and declare them all accessories to the Devil's work. I can't see any way around that. But don't worry – once he takes you away from here, they couldn't be held responsible."

Perfect and Pip looked at him with big eyes.

"He's going to take Pip away?" squeaked Perfect. "But … where?"

"He'll head for Ely, most likely," said the Traveler.

"What's going to happen to me there?" asked Pip, in a small voice.

"Nothing," said the Traveler. "Because he's not going to get you that far. Because we're not going to let him. With the team of the Traveler and Perfect – "

"That's Perfect and the Traveler," interrupted the gargoyle.

The man grinned and made a mock bow. "Of course. What was I thinking? With the team of Perfect and the Traveler on your case, we'll have come up with the solution to your problem before you can say *the Hunter outfoxed!"*

"What are you going to do?" asked Pip.

"We're going to make a happy ending."

"But … how?"

"Oh, I never reveal the details of a plan beforehand!" said the Traveler, with a confident laugh.

I expect that means you don't actually have one yet, thought Pip to himself, and then wished he hadn't. He wanted desperately to believe that the Traveler was going to make everything all right. The man didn't seem to notice the look of doubt on the boy's face, and settled himself comfortably, leaning back against a goat.

"Meanwhile," he said, "since nothing can be done just yet, and since you might, for no reason mind you, be ever so slightly keyed up – we thought we'd come and keep you company, and I'd tell you a story. To pass the time."

Pip appreciated the Traveler trying to cheer him up, but he was really not in the mood.

"Thanks, but I don't much feel like a story just now," he said, as nicely as he could manage.

The Traveler just looked at him. "Not even the story of why the good Radulfus has such an interest in me?" he asked. "Or the story of the Witch Bell?"

In spite of himself, Pip sat up straight in the straw. "The Witch Bell?!" he squeaked, but the Traveler raised a hand.

"One story at a time, young Pip, one story at a time!" He shifted some straw around into a more comfortable heap, and began.

"You may have guessed that I'm not an entirely honest man. I like to think I'm quite likeable – "

"Positively charming, I'd say," put in Perfect.

The Traveler acknowledged the compliment with a modest wave and continued. "And one of the reasons people like me is I like to give people what they want. If they want to smile, I tell them a joke. If they want sympathy, I listen to their sorrows. It's just the way I am. One day, I met a certain Abbot who wasn't looking for a joke or a sympathetic ear. What *he* wanted was to acquire a holy relic, something to make his abbey worth visiting, especially by wealthy, generous pilgrims. Something like, say, the thumb bone of Saint Neot. He wanted the thumb bone – I wanted him to have what he wanted – and so, I sold it to him."

"You had a saint's thumb bone with you, just like that?!" exclaimed Pip.

"Well, no. I had the thumb bone of a pig. Insofar as pigs have thumb bones. But you've no idea how happy it made the Abbot to think he'd bought a bit of a saint. And the donations from pilgrims – made happy by *seeing* a bit of a saint – practically doubled overnight. And *I* was happy to have my fee. So happiness all around, which is, I believe, God's wish for his children."

Pip couldn't believe the Traveler had gotten away with this. "So what happened?" he asked. "Did the Abbot find out you'd sold him a fake relic?"

"Not right away. Not even after I sold another thumb bone of Saint Neot to the Prior of another monastery (leagues and leagues from the first one, I assure you!) who also wished to encourage donations. It was only when I, foolishly I admit, sold a *third* thumb bone, that my luck ran out … No one would deny that Saint Neot was a remarkable man, but he did *not* have three thumbs."

Pip had to laugh. "Didn't you think anyone would notice?!" he exclaimed.

The Traveler scuffed his toes in the straw, looking for all the world like a boy caught stealing apples. "They never would have if it weren't for our interfering friend Radulfus," he rumbled.

"The Envoy?"

"Oh yes. Sadly, he's always been a man who could add two and one and come up with one too many. He's as much a traveler as I am, and it just so happened that he remembered seeing the first two thumbs. He noticed almost immediately the difficulty with the third. And so … "

"He started hunting for you?" asked Perfect.

"He did. He traced me from court to abbey to hovel to court. Up until now, I've always tried to make sure I was far enough ahead to do a bit of business before he could catch up with me at any point. Partly that's so I can make a living, partly it's because I like to think it keeps his heart beating fast and strong when he finds out about it! As I said, I like to give people what they want, and the Special Envoy is not a man who likes to be bored."

Just like you! thought Pip with a smile, but he didn't say it out loud. He didn't think the Traveler would appreciate the comparison.

Then something else came clear in his mind.

"So the bell you gave me, up on the tower – that was a fake too, I guess."

But Pip was wrong.

"Ah," said the Traveler, and his voice changed. "That's a different story. For me, especially. Do you remember the tale Walter told, about the sunken abbey and the skeleton monks?"

Pip and Perfect nodded.

"Well … I know how that story ends."

And he told Pip and Perfect how he had stumbled across the ruined abbey as it rose out of the marsh. How he had heard the Witch Bell ringing, and seen the dead brothers answer its call.

"At first, I screamed. I admit it. I was terrified! But for some reason I still don't understand, I didn't try to get away. I stayed and stared … "

And somehow – he couldn't explain! – he'd seen the great sorrow in the bell-ringer's face, and the yearning to be at peace, and when the monk held the bell out towards him, he'd known what to do, as clearly as if the dead man had spoken to him.

"I took the bell and I muffled it. And I'm almost certain that, in the silence that followed, I heard them all sigh. I know they were dead and so had no breath to sigh *with*, but that's what it sounded like. A great sigh of contentment. And then it all just crumbled away."

"What – the monks?" whispered Pip.

"And the abbey – everything just disappeared. Everything, except the bell."

"And you brought that away with you."

The Traveler nodded. "It seemed the right

thing to do," he said.

"You brought a Witch Bell to Wickit?" said Pip. "You gave me a cursed bell to ring?!" He didn't know whether to be furious or afraid.

The Traveler stirred impatiently. "You're as bad as Radulfus! That bell's no more cursed than our Perfect here. Not anymore. Maybe it's got an unusual history, but then so does she. The bell's just a bell, now that the brothers are at peace. They got their happy ending. And I, a seller of fake relics and lies, took part in a miracle." The lamplight showed a look of wonderment on his face, and then he shook himself and stood up. "You'll just have to trust me" he said briskly. "And that's enough storytelling for tonight! Some sleep is what we all need. I'll keep young Perfect with me for now – we don't want the Envoy getting his hands on her!"

It was true. Reluctantly, Pip said goodbye to the gargoyle and handed her over. He listened as the Traveler gave him some advice on how to act at the trial, and how he was not to worry, and how the rescue plan would most likely take place just when he was least expecting it! And then, having doused the lantern, they slipped out into the night as silently as they'd come.

The Traveler was a persuasive talker, and the

visit from him and Perfect had lifted Pip's spirits more than he realized. For a few moments after they'd left, he managed to hold onto that feeling. But then he remembered the look in the Envoy's black, dead eyes, and hope shriveled. A happy ending this time would be a miracle indeed! He'd never been in danger like this before – and the Abbey! What would happen to Wickit – would the Envoy punish his friends as well? There were so many horrors in his mind he thought he'd never sleep, and yet his body had other plans. The cold and wet, and the excitement and hard labor of the long night had worn him out. He snuggled down in the straw between the two warm goats and, suddenly and deeply, fell asleep.

On Trial!

The Envoy's man, still bleary-headed from the drugged drink, came into the shed the next morning. But before he could do more than shake his prisoner awake, Brother Barnard shouldered past into the warm, goat-smelling space, carrying a bowl of hot pottage.

"What's that for?" asked the man gruffly. "Devils don't eat. Not pottage, anyway."

"But boys do," retorted Brother Barnard. "Tuck in, Pip."

Pip did his best, but his throat was so tight it was hard to swallow.

"Never mind," the Cellarer said, taking the bowl back again and shoving away the interested noses of Blossom and Eloise. "You can have the rest when this silliness is over. We'll all have better appetites then." And he gave the Envoy's man such a look that the fellow gulped.

With Brother Barnard's red-faced presence treading on his heels, the serving man led Pip across the yard and towards the church, more gently than he might otherwise have done. For the first time in weeks, a watery sun had broken through the clouds, and the sight of it lifted Pip's spirits a little. But then, as they came through the church door, he stopped short, appalled, and had to be dragged forward.

The church was packed! It looked as if almost every inhabitant of Wickit was there.

"They've all come to see you acquitted," boomed Brother Barnard, but Pip wasn't so sure. The tiny amount of pottage in his stomach felt like a rock. He couldn't bear to look into the surrounding faces for fear of what he might see. Head down, he stumbled forward.

"That's far enough," said a voice. It was Radulfus. He was standing, his back to the altar. Abbot Michael and the Brothers had been relegated to one side, as if they were of no importance in their own church. The Envoy was holding a beautifully bejeweled cross, and wearing a robe of fine black wool that must have cost a fortune. Pip was immediately conscious of the state his own clothes were in after a night with the goats.

For a long moment, the Holy Hunter fixed the prisoner with his relentless, pitiless eyes, and watched him squirm.

Then the trial began.

"With God's blessing, I will now make my formal accusation." The Envoy's voice rang out, rich with authority and complete conviction. "I accuse this boy of being in league with the Devil. I saw him with my own eyes raise hellfire in the teeth of the storm, conjure up a Witch Bell, and consort with a fire-breathing imp, familiar or minor demon. The aim of these activities was to summon up Satan, the Master of all evildoers. And he did these deeds of darkness not in some unhallowed place, but most blasphemously on the tower of this very church." He looked at Pip in much the same way he would have looked at half a worm in an apple. "Do you have anything to say?"

Immediately a panicked jumble of words tried to fight their way out of Pip's mouth, but the Traveler had told him to say as little as possible. He'd said anything Pip said would only be twisted and distorted and used against him. Nothing he could say could make any of it any better.

It was true. There was nothing he could say. All he could do was stay silent, and try to be brave.

Pip bit his lips and closed his eyes tight, willing as much bravery into his heart as he could find …

Then his eyes jerked open again as, with an enormous crash, the door of the church slammed open, and the sunlight poured in. The cloaked and hooded figure of a man stood silhouetted in such brightness that, for eyes dazzled by the sudden light, it was impossible to tell who it was. He took a step forward, but his face was still obscured by the hood.

When he spoke, it was in a voice that dripped scorn.

"Call yourself a Holy Hunter? When you can't tell the difference between a decoy and the real prey?!"

Then was a moment of stunned silence, and then, "*You?!*" gasped the Special Envoy of the Church. "All the while, it was *you*?!"

Chapter 14

Revelation

It was the Traveler. As he pushed back his hood, he gave the Special Envoy a seriously disrespectful smile.

"That's right," he said. "All this time, it was me."

The Traveler recognized the sudden flare of excitement in his enemy's eyes, because he knew his man better than anyone. He knew how he thought, how he felt. He knew how it must have offended the Hunter's sense of his own importance, to be spending his considerable expertise on a peasant brat. But here, now, was an adversary worthy of him!

"Right here," the Traveler continued, "right

under your famous nose – I guess *that's* not something you'll want a lot of people to find out about, eh, Radulfus? Wouldn't do your reputation any good at all. You've chased me now from one end of the country to the other – and halfway across Europe before that – and then, when you're as close as you've ever been, you can't see for looking. I've grown extremely weary, waiting for you to realize the situation, so now I chose that you *should* see. Both me and – oh, and I don't think you've met … my familiar!" And with a flourish, he produced Perfect from under his cloak.

Everyone gasped at the sight of her, Pip as much as anybody. He had never seen her look so astonishing!

The Traveler had made her a beautiful, red wing cape, with fluttery, red ribbons. He'd managed to tie little red horns onto her head. She was even clutching a miniature pitchfork in her front paws. She looked every inch a tiny devil.

For a long moment, the Traveler let everyone look their fill, then he gave the gargoyle a tickle under her chin. Perfect suddenly tipped back her head and shot a bright burst of flame over the heads of the crowd! Everyone ducked, and there was more than one suppressed shriek.

The Traveler laughed, and placed the gargoyle onto his shoulder with a flourish. In spite of all the danger and fear, it was hard for her not to grin with excitement.

Radulfus started to take an eager step forward, but the Traveler raised his hand. "A moment, please," he said. "With your permission, I've first to deal with a slight staffing problem." His manner and tone would not have been out of place in a king's court, and the Envoy reluctantly responded with a curt bow.

The Traveler bent his head in return and then, so abruptly that everyone jumped, he turned and barked at Pip. *"You! Come here – and bring my bell!"*

Instinctively, Pip found himself obeying the voice of command. He scooped the bell off the altar, cradling it in his arms so that it wouldn't sound, and walked forward. The Envoy's man made a half-hearted move to stop him, but for the most part, Pip was aware of the crowd pulling back hurriedly as he passed. A random thought came into his mind, that the ones nearest the walls must be getting thoroughly squished. And then he was standing in front of the Traveler, and he could think of nothing else. There was something like a bubble of excitement around the man, an enormous alive-ness. He held his audience effortlessly, and reveled in the exercise of his skill. He looked at Pip, but his voice carried to the furthest corner of the church.

"There was a time when I thought you might be a recruit to the Devil's side of things, but" – and he shook his head in mock regret – "I was wrong. I should have realized you'd be unacceptable. My Master has no time for stupidity. Let Heaven be filled to the brim with all the stupid people of the world – Hell has higher standards!"

He turned away with a great, scornful whirl of his cloak while, out of sight of the crowd, he flicked a handful of something directly into Pip's face. Pip thought he might just have heard the man murmur, "Sorry about this," before his face suddenly felt as if it had been set on fire!

His eyes burned – his nose streamed – his throat went raw – and he started to sneeze uncontrollably.

"What have you done to him?" Abbot Michael cried, rushing forward, but the Traveler held up a commanding hand.

"Don't go near him, any of you! It is my Master leaving him. Everyone knows what a fit of sneezing means! Hear me, all of you – and you,

Hunter, most of all. The boy was bewitched but was found unworthy. When the sneezing passes, he will be as he was before – a sheep found too insignificant to be numbered among the goats!"

The two men locked eyes for a long moment, until Radulfus gave a nearly imperceptible nod. Only then did the Traveler back away, leaving the boy in a wheezing heap on the stone floor. Pip saw what happened next through a blurry haze of tears …

The Traveler had positioned himself with his back to the door, facing the Hunter. On either side, keeping as far away from either man as possible, were the Brothers and the Fen folk.

"And now," said the Traveler, with a half-hidden smirk, "I understand you wished to speak with me? I'm sorry if you've had difficulty catching up with me. I've been quite busy."

Perfect let out a sudden, high-pitched giggle (partly because she knew that eel-gutting right there on Wickit was one of the things he'd been busy with, but mainly from sheer nervousness). The sound hit Radulfus where it hurt. He flushed an angry red and his grip on the cross tightened until his knuckles showed white.

"Gloat all you like," he snarled. "It's true

you've escaped me before – but I have you now. Your powers are weakened inside this holy building. The Witch Bell will be useless to you here." He took a step forward and then another, holding the cross out in front of him. "Your Master, the Devil, the Evil One, cannot come to your rescue now … "

As he was speaking, the Traveler began to change, right in front of them. He seemed to be hunching in on himself, and there was suddenly an expression of evil on his face that Pip had never seen before. It was so strong that even the Envoy paused, disconcerted for a second.

And in that moment of hesitation, the Traveler took Perfect from his shoulder and threw her high into the air. All eyes followed her instinctively, except Pip's. While everyone else was transfixed by the aerial display of a small, winged demon, Pip watched the Traveler. He saw him slip a small, strange bundle made of reeds out of his cloak, letting it fall to the ground at his feet. And all the while he was calling out to Perfect in a voice unlike his own, higher, harsher, more than a little mad-sounding.

"Fly, my beauty, fly!" he shrieked. "See how they cower before you! Puny humans – it's true we cannot harm them, but our Master will rescue us

– I will call him to us – come, let us leave all this behind!" He swung his arm in a mighty arc and the bell rang, loud and clear and compelling. At the sound of it, most of his audience dropped onto their knees in terror, and Perfect swooped, flaming a tight, intense, focused fire …

A clap of thunder, unbearable in the enclosed space, shook the church. There was a flash of blue lightning, and a horrible, brimstone-smelling smoke billowed up. No one dared move in the murk. The air was filled with stifled shrieks and prayers and choking.

At first no one could see anything or anyone, but then the stinking smoke cleared a little and Radulfus burst through the open door into the sunlight – straight into Granny Groan, who was apparently on her way to see what all the excitement was about.

"You there, old hag!" shrieked the Hunter. "Tell me, where did he go? What did you see?"

Everyone came streaming out of the church behind him, including Abbot Michael who at once put a restraining hand on the Hunter's arm. "Gently, Envoy," he cautioned. "Granny's practically blind – chances are she won't have seen anything!"

Granny squinted out from the shawls around

her head at the sound of a familiar voice. She looked exactly like a cheerful gnome.

"Good day to you, Father!" she cried. "I don't think I know this other gentleman, but good day to him, too! What was it you were asking me? You must realize that what the good Father says is indeed the truth of it, for I'm not as cleverly-sighted as in my younger days – and I'm not sure what it is you think I *would* have seen if I *was*, if you follow my meaning. But there was *something* I noticed just now … "

"What? What?" demanded the Envoy.

The old woman lowered her voice, but only a little. "Well," she said, "I *did* notice a really rather

powerfully bad … smell. Now don't be offended, and I only mention it because I couldn't help wondering, you seeming quite an *excitable* sort of gentleman, well, as I say I just wondered … *Was it you, Your Honor?*" Her voice was a piercing whisper by this point, which meant that it reached every ear in the crowd with ease. Unaware of the almost purple color the Envoy's face had now turned, she carried on confidentially, "I only ask because the good Brother Gilbert gave me some medicine once when I was suffering from a similar condition and … I'm sorry, sir, I didn't hear – what was that you said?"

But the Envoy for some reason decided not to repeat his words. Instead he gathered his dignity around him like a cloak and addressed the gawping crowd.

"My work here is done," he announced solemnly. "All of you are witness to what you have seen here today, how the Devil was cast out of an innocent boy, and how the man of evil and his ghastly imp were sucked back into hell. I have defeated Satan on every front today, and now – I cast out his cursed bell as well!"

And without considering the danger to himself, the Envoy turned to where the Witch Bell lay forgotten on the ground, grasped it by its handle, took three giant strides towards the shore and flung it, high and hard, out over the flood. It rang three times as it flew, three perfect notes before it hit the water with a splash and a clang, and sank without trace. Silence pooled out from the place like ripples, and for a long moment no one spoke or seemed to breathe.

Then the Holy Hunter bent one expensively-clad knee, right there in the mud, prayed briefly, straightened, and walked away.

Later, at the evening meal, some of the Fen folk questioned Granny Groan about the whiff of brimstone she'd smelled outside the church, only to be told in no uncertain terms to stop talking nonsense. Granny Groan said she'd been nowhere near the church. She'd spent the whole day in the goat shed with Blossom, who had a tummy upset.

"If I didn't know better, I'd say someone'd been deliberately feeding her fennel," Granny said, with a most uncharacteristically tart note in her voice, "though I've made it known to all the world that her system can't abide it, in spite of the good it does for human stomachs. But then," and here her good nature re-asserted itself, "no one would do anything so wicked, would they. Not to such a lovely creature as my Blossom, the best of goats. Her tummy upset just must be from being away from home. It seems to be having an odd effect on all of us … "

Unexpected Presents

The fact that the flood waters began to ebb away, from that very day, was no surprise to Radulfus. It was the least he would expect, as an acknowledgement of the good work he'd done.

To everyone else, the speed at which the water receded was practically miraculous. It was as if the wet part of creation had suddenly shrugged and given up on its plans to take over the world. The sky cleared, a pleasant spring sun broke through, and a balmy spring breeze ruffled the reed beds. Sooner than anyone (except the Church's Envoy) would have thought possible, the water level of the Fens had dropped to a point at which it was safe for the refugees to venture home again. Some of the punts had been damaged or lost in the final storm, but by doubling up, neighbors were able to help each other on their way. With many cries of thanks, Wickit's flock scattered. The Holy Hunter went too, no longer intent on reaching Ely, but instead heading back the way he'd come. There would no doubt be a new mission for him and his nose soon enough, but he was just human enough to hope it wouldn't be *too* soon.

Pip, meanwhile, was keeping a very low profile. Being on trial for your life takes it out of you a bit, he'd found. And he couldn't help guessing that Prior Benet was rather disappointed in the outcome … He wondered where Perfect and the Traveler were hiding, but he was content to wait for a while to find out.

But then something extraordinary – *another* something extraordinary! – happened. As Pip and the Brothers came out of the church after Prime, they stumbled over a bundle left on the step.

"Not another orphan!" shrieked Prior Benet without thinking, and then blushed red.

It wasn't another orphan. As Brother Paul unwrapped the cloth, there was a faint chiming sound.

Everyone gasped as the metal of a bell gleamed in the sunlight.

"It can't be … !"

"But he threw it away … !"

"Careful – watch out … !"

But it was too late. Brother Paul let his arm drop and then brought it up again in a rich, full ringer's arc. The bell rang out, loud and clear, and there wasn't a soul who heard it who didn't smile. It was impossible to believe this was an evil, cursed Witch Bell. The Brothers passed it around, examining it carefully.

It was beautiful. And it was just what Wickit needed.

"It *couldn't* be the same bell," said Brother John, longingly. "We all saw the Special Envoy throw that other one away. This must just be *another* bell."

"It certainly makes a more suitable sound than that wretched bucket," muttered Prior Benet.

"I'm sure the Witch Bell was bigger than this one," said Pip. "I definitely remember it being bigger."

Prior Benet scowled at him for speaking on a matter that was none of his concern, but he nevertheless didn't disagree with what he'd said.

"That *proves* it's not the same bell, if the other

bell was bigger!" continued Brother John, in his eager voice.

"I'll pray on it," said Abbot Michael, with a smile. "But I'm hopeful we may have our bell problem miraculously solved."

The Brothers hoped so too, as they headed off to their various jobs.

"I'll just go and check the eel traps, shall I?" said Pip casually, to no one in particular. He wanted to be away from Wickit for a while. He knew now that there was some place (and it wasn't the eel traps) that he really needed to visit.

Because Pip had noticed something the Brothers hadn't.

Wrapped in with the bell was a fragment of dried-up peat, the sort of thing you'd find scattered around an old, no-longer-used, peat bed. Perhaps a peat bed with a deserted hut nearby. Where someone who for some reason didn't want to be conspicuous might stay for a while …

There was no sign of any life around, as Pip punted up to the old peat-cutter's hut. The damage from the flooding showed clearly on the deserted building, which was tilting dangerously towards collapse. It was a dreary place, just waiting to be claimed back by the marsh mud.

"Ah, I see you got my message!" said a voice from behind him.

Pip swiveled around, only just saving himself from tipping into the chilly water. There was the Traveler, sitting casually in one of the missing punts and smiling.

"Yes," Pip said. "I got your message." Suddenly, for no reason at all, he felt shy. "I … I wanted to thank you. You saved my life. And I wanted to ask you … " He trailed off, but the Traveler gave him an encouraging look.

"You wanted to ask me what?" he said.

Pip took a deep breath. "Why did you do it?" he asked quietly.

The man thought for a moment, and then shrugged. "I've no idea," he said. "Unless it was a miracle. Perhaps that was the third miracle I've been waiting for!"

He drew his punt alongside Pip's. "And speaking of miracles, I think I have something here that belongs to you," he said, and he reached into one of his pockets and drew out Perfect, who leaped with a small, happy cry, straight at Pip.

"Some*thing*?! You rude man!" she scolded

back at the Traveler from her boy's arms.

"Ah, Perfection," he said. "What a team we could have made, you and I." There was only a wisp of a question in his voice. He knew an unbreakable friendship when he saw one.

"And did the Brothers find a way to keep my present to them?" he continued. "I wish I could have heard how they convinced themselves! But I'm sure you helped."

Pip laughed. "I said it couldn't be the Witch Bell because I thought that was bigger, and pretty soon that was how everybody remembered it too. But how did you find it?! I thought it was gone for good!"

"Oh, I just came back in the night and used my demonic powers – with some help from my little familiar who has the most phenomenal diving skills!" Perfect looked smug. "Actually," the Traveler went on, "I just made sure I was paying attention when the Envoy chucked it into the marsh. And it wasn't easy with Granny Groan's old shawl falling over my face all the time! Anyway, I saw where it went under, and then we came and got it back again. I thought it was the least I could do for good old Wickit, for getting the Holy Hunter off my back for once and for all! And listen, I wanted to say … you know I never meant it, back there, when I called you stupid. I'm really sorry – and I'm sorry about the pepper too!"

Pip grinned ruefully. "You should be sorry! Next time you try a trick like that on me … well, just don't! Though it's really Brother Barnard you should apologize to – do you have any idea how much all that pepper cost?!"

The Traveler grinned, made a graceful gesture of apology and then reached for his boat's pole. Perfect gave an inadvertent whimper and Pip put a hand on the other punt's gunwale.

"You could come back with us, you know," he said earnestly. "The Hunter thinks he's sent you back to the Devil – he didn't even bother to carry on to Ely – and even if he hadn't given up on hunting you, Wickit would be the last place he'd look for you now." Even as he said it, Pip knew it would never work. But for the moment, he chose to ignore the small mountain of problems that would arise out of trying to shoehorn someone last seen disappearing into Hell into a monastic community.

"Tempting," the Traveler admitted. "And cunning as well. But I think, one way and another, I've had my three miracles. Besides, if I stayed, someone would probably want to give me a name. I'm not at all sure I'd like that, after all these years of doing without."

Then, suddenly, he froze.

"Did you hear that?" he whispered. "Did you hear someone out there?"

Perfect looked startled. "*I* didn't hear anything!" she said loudly, "and gargoyles have exceptional hearing ... " but Pip shushed her.

"Perfect and I'll go and look, shall we?" he asked. "Better safe than sorry." He offered the gargoyle his sleeve, and still looking unconvinced, she slid out of sight.

Pip took his time, and did an extra careful search of the surrounding marsh. But they found no one. And when they returned to the peat bed, the Traveler and his punt were nowhere to be seen.

"You don't look surprised," scolded Perfect. They'd gone over to the hut, and she'd peered and pried into the damp, dark, obviously empty corners, as if a grown man could hide under three rotten reeds and a broken cup. "Where's he gone? He can't be gone! He didn't say goodbye!"

Pip stroked her hard little head. "I think it was what he wanted," he said. "I don't think he much likes goodbyes."

She still seemed angry and sad, so Pip tried

one more thing.

"He left you a present, though," he said. "Would you like to have it now?"

Perfect tried hard to go on looking miffed, but curiosity got the better of her.

"A present? What is it?" she chirped.

And Pip showed her where the beautiful, red-ribboned wing cape had been hung on a peg just inside the door, where they couldn't help but see it as they left. Perfect held up her chin and he tied it on, took her into his hands, stepped outside into the late afternoon light and launched her. Her flight in the church had been constrained by ceilings and walls, but here she had the whole Fen sky to fly in. Ribbons fluttering wildly, she looped and soared, swooped and swirled, looking just like a bit of the sunset set free.

"Look at me! Look at me!" she squealed.

So Pip, his heart full, did.

The World of Wickit

Stranger than fiction, weirder than fantasy!

The Keeper of the Wickit Chronicles Answers Your Questions

What's Prime? And what are Matins and Lauds?

Prime was the first daylight service that the monks attended, but they'd already been up in the night for the prayers called Matins and Lauds. You had to be tough to be a monk.

What song was it that Perfect's Maker and the Traveler liked to sing?

The words of the song are in one of the medieval dialects of Venice, but translated into English, they begin:

Too much trust may place one in jeopardy! (Per tropo fede talor se perìgola!)

The song goes on to say that it's unfair the way people often pay no attention at all to our good deeds, while our mistakes get talked about thoroughly. *Then* it says how rotten it is when you love someone and they let you down. You might ask why these two men both had the same favorite song, all about what can happen when you get misjudged, and things go wrong in love. I don't know the answer, but I expect it wasn't just because they liked the tune.

If the Traveler really had the Plague, what would Brother Gilbert have done about it?

Nobody in Pip's time knew for certain what caused the Plague, and nobody knew for certain how to cure it. Brother Gilbert would likely have taken a number of different approaches all at once, in the hope that *something* might work.

He might have used a sharp knife or leeches to bleed his patient, because some people believed that disease was caused by an imbalance in the body and if you let some of the blood out, you might be able to bring things back *into* balance.

Or he might have prescribed any number of herbs or spices, such as ginger or valerian or borage. Borage was a useful ingredient in any Plague medicine because it was also thought to be good for melancholy, and finding out that you had the Black Death was enough to bring down anybody's mood.

Brother Gilbert would be unlikely to offer his patients powdered emeralds or molten gold to drink, since Wickit didn't have that kind of money available to it, but he could have given the dried toad approach a try … For this one, you need to dry a number of dead toads in the sun, and then place them on the Plague victim's boils. When the toads swell up and burst, just put on another one. Continue until the patient gets better, or you run out of toads.

You might ask if *any* of these cures worked, and the quick answer would have to be, well, no. Not really. Some people just got better by themselves, but it was pretty rare.

Was despair really considered a sin in medieval times?

This is a tough one. The reasoning went like this: if you really had given up all hope, then you must not believe in the goodness and mercy of God, and that was a sin. So, on top of feeling depressed, the despairing monks would also have the guilt of having sinned to cope with. It seems unfair to us, but that's how it seemed to them.

What's a brazier?

It may sound like medieval underwear, but it was in fact a handy metal basket on legs for burning wood or coal in. Unlike a built-in fireplace, it could be carried around, and used indoors or out.

What's a relic?

A relic is something that medieval people thought of as holy because it was associated with a holy person who had died. It could be something the holy person owned, like a shoe or a shirt, or it could be a part of their body, like a tooth or a bone. Churches would pay good money to have relics because pilgrims would be more likely to come to pray and make donations if there was something for them to see and marvel over when they got there.

The Traveler was not alone in trying to meet demand by embroidering the truth. Fake relics were big business in his time.

What's pottage?

Breakfast would normally have been a chunk of dark bread and a mug of ale, but on this occasion Brother Barnard thought Pip could do with something hot and more sustaining. Pottage was a bit like a soup, a bit like a stew. It was oat-based, but with all sorts of things added, depending on what was available at that season. The cook would add beans and peas, turnips and parsnips, leeks, cabbage, lettuce, onions, garlic, sometimes fish or meat – and I'd be very surprised if the occasional bit of eel didn't find its way into the pottage pot as well!

What's a familiar?

A familiar is an imp or minor demon who hangs out with a witch or wizard. They are usually in the shape of animals. Black cats are a favorite, but a familiar can be anything – an owl, a dog, even a ferret. Their main job is to help their mistress or master in doing evil, but I suspect they also provided much needed companionship.

What's so important about sneezing?

It's hard to get one clear story on what the significance of a sneeze was in medieval times. Some people said "Bless you" when you sneezed, because they thought it meant there was a demon coming out of you.

This was obviously a good thing – a blessing. Other people thought a sneeze made your soul come out of you, just for a second, which left it vulnerable to the Devil. If that were the case, you needed the blessing to protect you, until your soul could safely get back inside again.

In Germany, instead of "Bless you" they say "*Gesundheit*" or "Good health" to somebody who sneezes. In Pip's time, sneezing was one of the first signs of Plague. It was also the first sign of lots of other things, of course, like a cold. Still, it seemed like a good idea to hope that any particular sneeze wasn't the beginning of the Black Death.

Why did the Traveler say that Pip was really a sheep, and not a goat? Why did medieval people think of goats and the Devil together?

There is a parable in the Bible where Jesus talks about dividing the good people from the bad people at the end of the world. He calls the good people sheep and the bad people goats. This is a hard parable to live down, and many goats don't even try.

There were many different ways of portraying the Devil in medieval art, but the pictures often had more in common with pagan mythology than with what's in the Bible. The image of Satan with goat's horns and hind legs, for example, looks a lot like the pagan god Pan, and the pitchfork idea may have come from the sea god Neptune's trident.

There were no guns at this time, so how would the Traveler have known about gunpowder? And why did it smell bad?

The Chinese invented gunpowder – there doesn't seem to be a lot that they *didn't* invent! – around 2,000 years ago, but of course, since guns didn't exist then, they didn't call it that. They called it *"huo yao"* ("Fire Chemical") and its main use was for making fireworks. Some historians think the recipe may have come to the west with Marco Polo, and then to England with returning Crusaders. The medieval friar Roger Bacon wrote about the "black powder" (in code, because he was pretty sure it would spell trouble, one way or another) and identified the three elements and their proportions. One of these, sulfur, makes a smell like rotten eggs.

It is not clear exactly how the

Traveler got the recipe or the ingredients, but he was a man who had seen quite a lot of the world. And who knows? He may even have met with Friar Bacon, and applied his considerable charm.

There are lots of polite ways of referring to "passing wind." Were there any medieval cures for, you know, flatulence?

"The expelling of wind" was a topic that got mentioned a fair amount by medieval medical types. To cure the condition, some recommended powdered bay leaf taken with honey. Others suggested feverfew fried with wine and oil and applied to the belly. Then there was also mint, valerian, hemp seeds, dill, anise seeds, cardamom seeds, fennel, cloves …

Something quite interesting about many of the cures for wind is the fact that they were also prescribed for Plague, the bite of a mad dog, and acne. The up side to this was that anyone unfortunate enough to have all those conditions at the same time wouldn't have to spend all day taking different medicines.

Who was Saint Neot?

Neot was a contemporary and, some say, friend of Alfred the Great. He is thought to have been only four feet tall.

He is the patron saint of fish ...

The World of Wickit ... like it says on the label, stranger than fiction, weirder than fantasy!